THE FOLLOWING MOVIE MYSTERY HAS BEEN APPROVED FOR

ALL AUDIENCES

BY THE GOOD PEOPLE AT WALKER BOOKS UK

THIS BOOK HAS BEEN RATED:

C	COSMIC
	SCENES OF AMERICAN AWESOMENESS, EPIC STUNTS AND ONE WEIRD CAT

2000652763

NEATH PORT TALBOT LIBRARIES

Also by Tanya Landman

SAM SWANN'S MOVIE MYSTERIES

ATTACK OF THE BLOBS!!!....

TANYA LANDMAN

ILLUSTRATIONS BY
DANIEL HUNT

WALKER
BOOKS

This is a work of fiction. Names, characters, places and
incidents are either the product of the author's imagination or,
if real, are used fictitiously. All statements, activities, stunts,
descriptions, information and material of any other kind
contained herein are included for entertainment
purposes only and should not be relied on for
accuracy or replicated as they may result in injury.

First published 2015 by Walker Books Ltd
87 Vauxhall Walk, London SE11 5HJ

2 4 6 8 10 9 7 5 3 1

Text © 2015 Tanya Landman
Illustrations © 2015 Jay Wright

The right of Tanya Landman to be identified as author of
this work has been asserted by her in accordance with the
Copyright, Designs and Patents Act 1988

This book has been typeset in Stempel Schneidler

Printed and bound in Great Britain by Clays Ltd, St Ives plc

All rights reserved. No part of this book may be reproduced,
transmitted or stored in an information retrieval system in
any form or by any means, graphic, electronic or mechanical,
including photocopying, taping and recording, without prior
written permission from the publisher.

British Library Cataloguing in Publication Data: a catalogue
record for this book is available from the British Library

ISBN 978-1-4063-5818-6

www.walker.co.uk

NEATH PORT TALBOT LIBRARIES	
2000652763	
PETERS	23-Dec-2016
JF	£5.99
BAG	

For Louise, Chris, Ruby, Marie and Stanley

All the chapters in this book are named after movies.
This is how I rate them:

SAM SWANN'S BOARD OF FILM CLASSIFICATION

BG — **BANNED BY GRAN**
(Unseen by Sam)

F — **FANTABALISSIMO**

FF — **FANTASTICALLY FANTABALISSIMO**

FFF — **FANTASMAGORICALLY FANTASTICALLY FANTABALISSIMO**

WTA — **WET THURSDAY AFTERNOON**
(Only watch if there's nothing better to do)

3A — **AVOID AT ALL COSTS**

W — **WEIRD**

RS — **RUBBISH SEQUEL**
(Watch the original instead)

5Z — **ZZZZZ**
(Sleep guaranteed)

EPS — **EYE-POPPINGLY SCARY**

WLI — **WATSON LOVES IT**

GGG — **GIGGLES GALORE GUARANTEED**

Watson
my brother-from-
another-mother

Me,
Sam Swann

My dad, **Marcus** –
special-effects make-up
artist to the stars

Gran
aka the
Big Boss

THE *PRIZE* ⒻⒻⒻ

Oscars night. It's the same every year. Me, Dad, Gran
and Watson huddle around the TV. Dad sits so close
to the screen that his nose is almost pressed against it,
and he bites his fingernails before each announcement.
If he likes the winner, he punches the air. If he doesn't,
he uses language I'm not even allowed to write down.

Dad gets super excited by The Oscars, but even
with all that glitz and glamour I think it's pretty dull.
A bunch of grown-ups patting each other on the
back, air-kissing and shrieking, "Darling, you were
marvellous!" BOR-RING!!!

A NIGHT AT THE OSCARS

There is a different movie star or celebrity to present each award.

Please welcome Cameron Diaz!

I'm delighted to present the award for Best Actor in a Leading Role.

The celeb lists the nominees for that category.

The nominees are: Rhys Evans for *My Green Valley*, George Kinsella for *The Lonesome Fisherman*, Antonio Little for *Mermaid Moon* and William Idaho for *Two Leaden Feet!*

Big build-up with drum rolls and music...

TV screen splits to show close-up of each nominee.

The winner gets their award.

Celeb opens envelope ...

And the winner is ...

... and reads out winner's name.

... George Kinsella for *The Lonesome Fisherman!!!*

The losers clap politely and try to look pleased, but you can tell what they're really thinking.

That is SO unfair!

He's RUBBISH!

It should have been me!

Dad would LOVE to get an Oscar nomination. It's been his ambition ever since he started working in the movie industry. So far, he's never even come close,

UNCLE OSCAR

Oscars are really Academy Awards, but in 1931 the Academy's Executive Secretary said that the winners' statuettes looked like her Uncle Oscar. That name stuck.

despite being a special-effects genius and "the besthe in the business" according to child superstar Tinkerbelle Cherry. So on Oscars night, when they announce the winner for Best Make-Up and Hairstyling, Dad gets a bit tetchy. In fact, mild-mannered Marcus Swann transforms into ... the Incredibly Jealous Hulk!!!

Dad's next film is called:

Not only does it have a megastar-studded cast, but also a director who's been nominated for Best Picture

FUR IN FILM

Uggie is the Jack Russell who starred in *THE ARTIST* and *WATER FOR ELEPHANTS*. The part of Toto in *THE WIZARD OF OZ* was played by a cairn terrier called Terry. She was paid $125 a week – more than some of the human actors.

three times and won twice. Dad is super happy because as well as having The L Factor in shedloads (i.e. it might get its own Lego range, like *THE LONE RANGER* or *THE HOBBIT*), the movie has O Potential (i.e. it could get nominated for a gazillion Oscars). OK, it will be ages before the film hits cinema screens, but I know that Dad is secretly hoping this will be The One.

Actually, that would be pretty cool. We'd get to go to the ceremony in Los Angeles and wear suits and ride in a limousine and strut up the red carpet getting snapped by paparazzi. They'd let Watson in, no trouble. After all, Uggie was there when *THE ARTIST* won.

ALIEN BG EPS

I have been attacked by an alien blob monster. It's squirted my face with toxic slime and my skin has started to boil. I'm covered in gigantic pus-filled blisters. It's gruesome. But hey, don't worry about me – I won't have to suffer for long. Any second now the blob will bite my head off and it will all be over!

The reason for this goo-filled zit-fest is that Dad is preparing for *ATTACK OF THE BLOBS!!!*

Zombies? Mummies? The living dead? Darling, they are sooooo last year! Which is just as well, because frankly I was sick to death of them. But this season's trend? It's out of this world, literally.

It's a sunny summer's day and I'm lying on the grass in Gran's back garden. Dad is peering at my face through a magnifying glass. He prods one of the pustules with his finger. It squelches noisily, then pops. Green slime oozes down the side of my neck and slowly drips onto the grass.

Dad is not happy. Very soon we're jetting off to America to begin filming. The blisters have to be just right before he can stick them on all the actors. So far they're not working the way he planned.

"That's no good," he says crossly, as if it's my fault. "Stay right there, Sam. I'll whip up a stronger mix."*

Stay right there. Brilliant. Hungry-looking crows line up on the garden fence, a menacing glint in their eyes. Where's my pack brother when I need him?

---

* See APPENDIX to find out how to making convincing rashes, zits and pus. (That's the section at the back of this book, not my insides.)
  NB Dad's secret recipe isn't there: if you read it, I'd have to kill you.

Out of the corner of my eye I can see my dog practising Jedi mind tricks. He figures that if Luke Skywalker could levitate a whole spaceship out of a swamp, he ought to be able to raise a few crusts off Gran's bird table. It hasn't worked yet, but he's a Labrador, and Labradors are Relentlessly Optimistic.

I'm feeling Relentlessly Optimistic too. I mean, Dad's next movie is going to be FANTABALISSIMO. The logline is:

CAPTAIN QUARK BATTLES HER ARCH-ENEMY GALAXION TO SAVE PLANET EARTH!!!

The stunt-a-second plot goes like this:

Ms Bosun-Higgs is a geeky particle physicist.

But she's also ... Captain Quark! A superhero from a galaxy far, far away.

In her lunch hour, Captain Quark is kept busy doing the usual super-hero stuff:

Stopping aeroplanes falling out of the sky ...

... dragging sinking ships safely to shore ...

... catching trains as they plummet off bridges.

But Captain Quark has a secret – she's hiding on Planet Earth from her evil twin and arch-enemy ...

GALAXION!!!

Things are going well until Bring Your Child to Work Day.

Ms Bosun-Higgs' handsome colleague Professor Goodheart brings his adorably cute niece Lucy-May to the lab.

Disaster strikes! While the grown-ups are flirting (euw!) the little girl wanders off.

She takes a wrong turn and goes through a door marked TOP SECRET.

Lucy-May spots a big red button and is unable to resist. She presses it.

This accidentally sets off a chain reaction ...

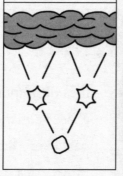

... that causes an explosion, sending shock waves right across the universe.

Galaxion intercepts them and traces the source to Earth.

The evil space traveller boards his spaceship and goes looking for Captain Quark.

MEET THE CAST

Felicia Luffman as
our epic superhero

CAPTAIN QUARK

George Kinsella as her
arch-enemy

GALAXION

Rhys Evans as
her love interest

PROFESSOR GOODHEART

Tinkerbelle Cherry as his
adorable orphaned niece

LUCY-MAY GOODHEART

It takes a while for Galaxion to reach Planet Earth, and, unaware that disaster is about to strike, Ms Bosun-Higgs and Professor Goodheart decide to take Lucy-May for a day out at Moviewonderland. The trio are happily watching the parade when Galaxion swoops down and snatches Lucy-May. Captain Quark flies off in pursuit. In an epic chase sequence they whoosh past every famous landmark in America, from Mount Rushmore and the Grand Canyon to Niagara Falls and the Empire State Building. They end up at the Statue of Liberty, where Galaxion uses the statue's famous torch as a transmitter (like in *MEN IN BLACK II*) to open a wormhole (like in *AVENGERS ASSEMBLE*), linking Earth with Galaxion's home planet. Alien blob monsters pour through, squirting slime and chomping people's heads off.

WALK LIKE A BUG

In the first *MEN IN BLACK* film, the actor who played Edgar the Bug wore knee braces and taped up his ankles so he could get a really good insect-like walk.

ATTACK OF THE BLOBS!!! is a guaranteed gazillion-dollar blockbuster, which involves:

A flying superhero	An evil baddie with cosmic powers	Radioactive blob monsters	Billions of explosions
☑	☑	☑	☑

What's not to like?

I'm still lying on the grass oozing when Gran gets home. She isn't pleased to find Dad in the kitchen using her brand-new blender to whip up pus. The whisk attachment is covered in green goo. She's even less pleased when she slips on the slime that's seeped onto the grass and goes skidding into the bird table. The only one who's happy is Watson.

His Relentless Optimism has finally been rewarded: he sincerely believes he's managed to levitate those crusts himself.

Wonderful. My dog now thinks he's a Jedi Master.

GOSSIP

Dad isn't the only one who's excited about *ATTACK OF THE BLOBS!!!* Filming hasn't even started, yet there's already a massive buzz about the movie online and in the media. The reason for the hype is that right after the Oscars ceremony something truly gross happened in Los Angeles.

> **Q**: Was it an earthquake?
>
> **A**: No!
>
> **Q**: Was it a plane crash?
>
> **A**: No!!
>
> **Q**: Were lots of fluffy animals in deadly danger?
>
> **A**: No!!! Worse. Much worse.

WARNING:
GRAB YOUR SICK
BUCKETS NOW!!!

Here's what happened: Felicia Luffman (aka Captain Quark) and George Kinsella (aka Galaxion) went to an after-show party. Their eyes met across a crowded room *(creepy music)* and then *(Dun, dun, DUN!!)*...

They fell deeply in **LURVE**.

Euw!

Not exactly headline news, you would think, yet somehow it pushed everything else off the front pages. I have NO idea why grown-ups are interested in this stuff, but there's been no getting away from it for weeks now. Stories about Felicia and George are EVERYWHERE. If they go shopping or out for a walk in the park, if they decide to have a burger or buy a toothbrush, they are followed by an army of photographers and journalists. What's more, anyone who gets anywhere near them blogs or tweets about it. The web is groaning under the weight of all the gossip.

Louisa @scratchmyback
Her nail varnish was pearly pink!

Georgie @twoleftfeet
His socks were green!!

Brian @bigfatfries
They had two burgers – one with gherkins, one without!!!

What's worse, the press have taken the two names and done something weird:

Felicia Luffman +
George Kinsella...?

Felicia Luffman
F. Luffman = Fluff

George Kinsella
Kinsella = Kins

Fluff + Kins = ?

NAME CHANGERS

Lots of film-star couples
are given new names
by the press, e.g.

Brad Pitt
+ Angelina Jolie
= Brangelina

Tom Cruise
+ Katie Holmes
= TomKat

You've guessed it! The loved-up couple are now known as ...

FluffKins

Double EUW!!

If you switch on the TV, you see this:

If you walk into a shop, you see this:

Hollywood **News**

Has George proposed?

EXPRESS

GEORGE SEEN SHOPPING FOR RINGS!

THE DAILY NEWS

FELICIA SAYS

YES!

STAR TODAY

Felicia's secret meeting with wedding planner!

If you turn on the radio, you hear this:

It's revolting. I hope they've got over themselves by the time filming starts, or the rest of the cast and crew will be like this:

MOVIEWONDERLAND

AMERICAN DREAMZ

Dad's shooting schedule reads like a list of every famous spot in America. And – get this! – the first location is Moviewonderland.

MOVIEWONDERLAND!

It's like Disney World, only a gazillion times better.

Cosmic Films are taking over the entire theme park to shoot the scenes where Lucy-May is snatched by Galaxion. I get to just hang out and try out all the rides. Can life get any better than this?

Gran takes us to the airport and waves us off. Underneath that brave smile she must be pretty jealous. I mean, we're going to MOVIEWONDERLAND!!!

I wasn't allowed to take my pack brother to Egypt when we filmed *TOMB OF DOOM!!!* because of the quarantine regulations, but they don't have the same rules in the USA. Watson has his own passport and has had all the right vaccinations (not that he thanked me for them).

As if the injections weren't bad enough, he has to fly to America in what the transport company calls a "sky kennel".* I feel really sorry for him. I don't see why my dog can't have his own seat in the cabin with us. It would make the flight a lot less boring.

But rules are rules. I'll just have to make it up to him when we get there.

---

* I call it a big crate.

Filming a movie can be pretty dull, but I'm sure *ATTACK OF THE BLOBS!!!* will be different. Me and Watson are going to have the best time ever. I'm home-schooled by Dad, who thinks this trip will be Highly Educational. He's expecting me to learn all about American history and culture. He's brought a whole briefcase full of lesson plans.

GEOGRAPHY

1. What is the largest state in the USA?

2. Which state is made up entirely of islands?

3. What is the highest mountain in the USA?

4. Where is Tornado Alley?

HISTORY

1. Where will you find the phrase *All men are created equal*?

2. Who said, "I have a dream"?

3. Who was shot dead on 22 November 1963?

I, meanwhile, have other ideas. Me and Watson have big plans.

My Yankee Doodle To-Do List

- Climb the Empire State Building
- Eat hot dogs
- And burgers
- Toast marshmallows
- Ride in a horse-drawn carriage around Central Park
- Go over Niagara Falls in a barrel
- Watch a baseball match
- Drive across the Brooklyn Bridge in a yellow taxi
- Gallop through the Grand Canyon like cowboys
- Go surfing like cool dudes
- Go skateboarding like even cooler ones
- Learn to breakdance

This is going to be FFF.*

---

* FANTASMAGORICALLY FANTASTICALLY FANTABALISSIMO.

SCANDAL BG 5Z

We've checked in and are heading for the departure lounge when Dad suddenly stops dead and looks like this:

For a moment I can't work out what's happened to him. I put on my Sherlock Holmes hat and ask myself what could be the cause.

Electric shock?
Hit by lightning?
Zapped by alien blob monster?

Then I see what he's looking at.

GEORGE DEVASTATED!
Close friends of George Kinsella rushed to his side yesterday as the news of fiancée Felicia's cheating broke.

DISTRAUGHT FELICIA SAYS SHE'LL NEVER LOVE AGAIN!!
Sources close to Felicia Luffman describe her as an emotional wreck.

FLUFFKINS SPLIT!!!
Late last night, in a crowded Hollywood restaurant, a tearful Felicia broke down and sobbed, "George dumped me! How could he do this?"

All the way to America, Dad frets about the effect this will have on the shoot.

Will Felicia and George be able to work together?

Will they even be able to sit in Make-up at the same time?

Will they come to blows on set?

Will we be besieged by paparazzi?

Will I have to rearrange my entire schedule...?

I don't have a lot to say about it all, so instead I look at the magazine that's stuffed into the back of the seat in front.

From this, I learn how to translate English into American:

Lift	→ Elevator
Toilet	→ Bathroom
Tap	→ Faucet
Cupboard	→ Closet
Curtains	→ Drapes
Bin	→ Trash can
Garden	→ Yard
Sweets	→ Candy
Crisps	→ Chips
Chips	→ French fries
Candyfloss	→ Cotton candy
Trousers	→ Pants
Pants	→ Underwear
Trainers	→ Sneakers
Autumn	→ Fall*
Mad	→ Crazy
Angry	→ Mad

---

* This is what they call autumn because it's when the leaves fall off the trees. I wonder if they call winter "cold and damp"?

The flight is really long and west-coast American time is eight hours behind England, which means we leave at 10 a.m., fly for eleven hours and get there at 1 p.m. EH??!!

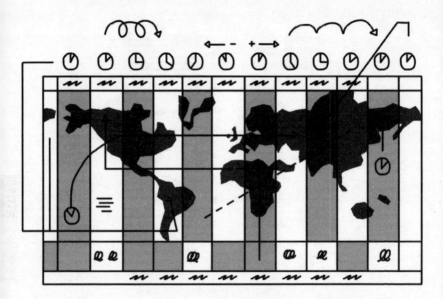

By the time we arrive, I'm exhausted – it's nearly bedtime in England but here in Los Angeles people are tucking into lunch. Weird. When we collect Watson, my pack brother is as confused as me.

We let him out of his sky kennel and stand well back, expecting high energy tail-wagging and canine cartwheels. But he's too sleepy. Instead, he sags onto the floor and I have to drag him to the waiting taxi. I can tell what he's thinking:

Time Zones
Because the earth spins around once every twenty-four hours, the sun shines on different bits of it at different times. So when it's midday in England it's midnight in New Zealand.

Isn't it bedtime?
It feels like bedtime!
But why is the sun
still in the sky?

When we get into the taxi, he climbs onto my lap and falls asleep.

Dad is the only one who isn't tired. He's still worrying about whether or not his pustules will

LOVE AND REMARRIAGE

There are some Hollywood couples who have got married, divorced and then married again – to each other. Richard Burton and Elizabeth Taylor did it. So did Natalie Wood and Robert Wagner, as well as Melanie Griffith and Don Johnson.

be up to the job. Plus he's really wound up about the whole FluffKins thing. Personally, I can't see the problem. The fact that the two lead actors are no longer all over each other will be a massive relief to everyone. Just as long as they don't do a Burton and Taylor and change their minds.

THE *BIG SLEEP*

It takes us about an hour to drive from the airport to Moviewonderland. When we pull up at the entrance I am officially Out Of It. Dad has to prod me and Watson to keep us awake. I want to go straight to bed but Dad won't let me.

"It's called jet lag, Sam. If you go to bed now, you'll be skipping around in the middle of the night when everyone else is trying to sleep and then you'll never get your body clock sorted. You need to stay awake for as long as possible."

> **Jet Lag**
> If you're on a long flight from east to west – or west to east – your body's natural 24-hour clock, which controls sleeping and waking patterns, gets disrupted. It can take a few days to adjust to a new time zone.

What's he on about? I've got a Body Clock? Who knew…?

We go into the meet and greet area, where a few people from the film are hanging around chatting or grabbing lunch from the buffet. Dad does a lot of high-fiving, Watson gets patted on the head and I get my hair ruffled. (Why do grown-ups do that?) Felicia is nowhere to be seen, but George Kinsella is talking to Rhys Evans (aka Prof. Goodheart).

George is pink-eyed and puffy, so I guess he's got jet lag too.

BORING!! Me and my pack brother follow Dad to the reception desk and collapse into a heap at his feet while he checks us in. We both start to doze. So Dad does this:

That is *definitely* cruelty to children. And animals! Dad threatens to make me and Watson run around the theme park until bedtime. But when he finally collects our room keys, there's a note waiting for us.

M O V I E W O N D E R L A N D
T H E   L A S T   R E S O R T

Message to: Mr Samuel Swann
From: Miss Tinkerbelle Cherry
Message content:
Miss Tinkerbelle Cherry requests your immediate presence in the Guinevere Suite.

CATS AND DOGS

Tink's note says that she "requests" my presence in
her hotel suite, but Dad and I know there will be
pouty lips, stamped feet and major sulking if we don't
get over there NOW!

While me, Dad and Watson are staying in one of
Moviewonderland's economy hotels, Tink is in their

most expensive one. She is, after all, Hollywood royalty.

We have a room in the saloon of the Wild West frontier town Desperation, which is comfortable enough but pretty basic. Tink, meanwhile, gets the Guinevere Suite in King Arthur's Castle in the Land of Legend. The castle looks pretty cool from the outside – it has a moat and a drawbridge and everything! – but when we get inside, I wonder, does anything get girlier than this?

Tink's my best friend (after Watson, obvs). She's very clever and brave but she has some weird ideas when it comes to leisure activities* – and as a Hollywood megastar, she can ask for anything her heart desires and the film company will do its very best to get it for her.

Up until now, Tink's contractual demands have included squadrons of Barbies, swarms of pink teddies and five real, live kittens for her to play with when she's not filming.

STORE CRAZY

One of the most famous movie hotels is *THE GRAND BUDAPEST HOTEL*, although the film was actually shot in a department store.

---

* Like playing with Barbie and Ken *all* the time.

But when we arrive at the Guinevere Suite we're faced with something entirely new. This isn't five kittens. This is just one THING.

I have no idea what it is.

Monkey?   Bat?   Gremlin?

You know how Disney's main characters always get an animal sidekick? Aladdin has Abu, the Little Mermaid has Flounder, Rapunzel has Pascal. The only one not to get an adorably cute companion is Lilo: instead, she gets landed with Stitch, a fantastically destructive alien. I know I'm jet-lagged, but for a moment I think Tink's managed to get hold of Stitch himself.

Dad goes off to chat to Tink's mum and I'm left alone with Tink and the creature from outer space.

She's squeezing the THING so tightly I'm amazed it doesn't pop. Its head is so small that between its massive ears there can't be any room for a brain. And the look in its eyes is distinctly unfriendly.

Watson, however, is a Relentless Optimist. When he sees it, he wags his tail so hard he bruises my legs.

Tink squeals and brings the THING over for me to get a better look.

THAM!

Meet my new pet! He's a Siamese kitten. His pwoper name is Pwince Wupert the Third, but I call him Woopie. Isn't he beautiful?

Er … no! The THING's clear blue eyes fix me and Watson with a killer glare. Prince Rupert III is possibly Evil Incarnate.

"Let's get Woopie and Watson pwoperly intwoduced," says Tink. "I know they'll be best fwends for ever. Just like you and me!"

The trouble with cats and dogs is that they don't speak the same body language. They just don't get each other. Dogs are pretty straightforward:

HOW TO MAKE FRIENDS: CANINE FASHION

But cats? Poor Watson is confused.

Tink puts Prince Rupert III down on the carpet. Watson sniffs his nose. Watson sniffs his bottom. Watson wags his tail.

---

* Why? Best not to think about it.

Prince Rupert wags his tail too, but I'm not convinced it means quite the same thing. This is what a tail wag means for:

A DOG

Hello, new-found friend! I love you. Let's play!

A CAT

I loathe and despise you, foul-smelling canine. If you persist in pressing your cold wet nose against my bottom, I shall be compelled to take drastic action.

When His Highness hisses and runs away, it very definitely *isn't* an invitation for Watson to play a lovely game of Chase Me Around The Guinevere Suite with Woopie.

But my dog thinks it is. And I'm on the end of his lead. This is what happens:

Luckily it doesn't take Watson long to run out of
energy and collapse in a panting heap.

I open my mouth to apologize, but Tink gives me
a LOOK. Those feline eyes of hers go into calculating
little slits and she says ever-so-sweetly, "Don't worry
about it, Tham. I'm sure you'll find a way to make it
up to me."

Uh-oh. I don't like the sound of that.

THE JUNGLE BOOK (FFF)

At 8 p.m. American time, I'm finally allowed to go to bed. That's 4 a.m. UK time. Four in the morning! Twelve hours later, I'm in the middle of a dream in which I'm being chased around King Arthur's Castle by Lilo and Stitch when thirty kilos of Labrador lands on my chest, slobbers all over my face and tells me (in Labradorian) that he's desperate to …

1) Wee
2) Poo
3) Eat breakfast
4) Eat more breakfast
5) Eat even more breakfast

… in that order. It's a brand-new day and Watson is bright-eyed, bushy-tailed and raring to go. I am not.

Dad's already gone off to work, leaving me a note. I expect it to be a list of schoolwork to do in his absence, but all it says is:

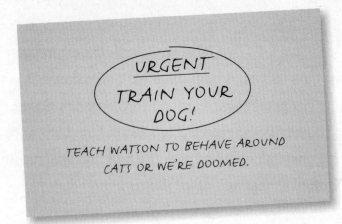

I crawl out from under the covers, and three minutes later my pack brother and I are walking the mean streets of Moviewonderland.

Route 66 is swarming with sparks* and stunt crew all setting up for the day's filming. They're starting with the scene where Galaxion swoops down over the carnival parade and snatches Lucy-May. In the movie it will look like this:

---

* That's film speak for the electricians.

#4792 The parade

Route 66, Moviewonderland.
The carnival is in full swing.

Camera zooms in for close-up of
Ms Bosun-Higgs watching the parade
with Prof. Goodheart and Lucy-May.

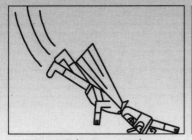

Horror! Galaxion swoops down.

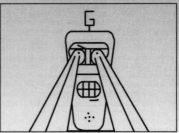

He beheads the parade's characters with
his laser-beam eyes – first King Arthur ...

... then Merlin ...

... Desmond, the flying dormouse ...

... and Pinkety-Boo.*

Galaxion's laser eyes search the crowd ...
and zoom in on Ms Bosun-Higgs.

His computer-like brain scans her to find her
point of weakness: Lucy-May.

He snatches the child and takes off!

Ms Bosun-Higgs transforms into
Captain Quark.

She flies in pursuit.

Right now, it looks like chaos and sounds like this:

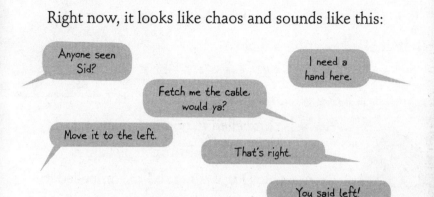

Anyone seen Sid?

I need a hand here.

Fetch me the cable, would ya?

Move it to the left.

That's right.

You said left!

All kinds of highly technical stuff is going on. The crew are setting up various cameras so that they can follow Galaxion when he swoops down over the crowd. The stunt co-ordinator, Barry Lasseter,** is double checking George's harness and rigs.

Me and Watson slip away, and before too long we find ourselves in the Jungle Zone – where we discover a lost temple, a snake pit, a crocodile lake, an Amazonian canoe ride and Tarzan's Tearooms. There is also plenty of vegetation, and as soon as I let Watson off the lead he

LONG SHOT

The first movie ever made in Hollywood was *In Old California*. Filmed in 1910, the shoot lasted only two days. Things have changed a bit since then. The record for the longest continuous film shoot stands at 400 days.

---

* Galaxion doesn't have to do this, he just slaughters people for fun. That's how bad he really is.

** He was also the stunt co-ordinator on *Zombie Dawn!!!*

disappears into some bushes,
looking over his shoulder
to check I'm not following.
He is a dog on a mission.

He feels compelled to poo in private, which
is understandable. Unfortunately, I am a
Responsible Dog Owner so I'm compelled to
follow.

I'm crawling through the bushes after him when
I hear someone sobbing. I peep through the leaves
and see Felicia (aka Ms Bosun-Higgs/Captain Quark)
sitting on a bench. She's crying her eyes out. Rhys
Evans (aka Professor Goodheart) is with her, looking
a bit uncomfortable. He has one
arm around her shoulder and is
patting her awkwardly. They're
whispering, but I don't know
why they bother: actors can't
help talking ten times louder than
normal people. It must be part of
their Thespian Training.

GREEK GUY

"Thespian" is a
fantastically fancy word
for actor. Thespis lived
in Ancient Greece and
was the first person to
play a character on
stage. He must have
learned to talk really
loudly, as they didn't
have microphones in
those days.

"FELICIA WAS THE GIRLFRIEND FROM HELL," SAYS GEORGE

```
Rhys:       I'm so sorry...
Felicia:    How could he say such
            things? I thought
            George was, you know,
            The One. How could he
            dump me?
Rhys:       I'm here for you. If
            you need a shoulder
            to cry on, I'm your
            man.
Felicia:    Oh, Rhys...!
```

She erupts into another fountain of tears. Honestly, actors! Why are they all such drama queens?

TRAINING DAY

Dad says I must TRAIN MY DOG. The trouble is, I can't really teach him to behave around cats without having a cat to practise on.

 I buy a fluffy toy cat from the Moviewonderland shop, which Watson snatches before running off. He shakes the thing until he's killed it stone-dead and then pulls all the stuffing out. This is not going to plan.

I assess the situation. As a minor,
Tink can only work for a certain number
of hours each day, then when her time is up
she leaves the set. If past experience is anything to
go by, one weird kitten and a Barbie army won't keep

 her busy for long. Soon I will be required
to Entertain her. That will be the time to
commence Canine Education
Exercises.

I check my watch. Lunchtime. Dad will be eating
on set, but Watson and I go for a Jungle
Burger and Amazonian Fries at Tarzan's
Tearooms. Sure enough, the minute we
get back to our room I am summoned
to the Guinevere Suite.

I go prepared. Gran gave me about

 a million books on dog training when
Watson was a puppy and I read every
single one. I know all about Positive
Reinforcement. It's

time to use the F word.*

---

* FOOD!!!

This is how it should work:

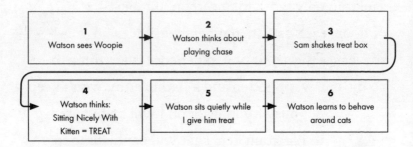

1 Watson sees Woopie	2 Watson thinks about playing chase	3 Sam shakes treat box
4 Watson thinks: Sitting Nicely With Kitten = TREAT	5 Watson sits quietly while I give him treat	6 Watson learns to behave around cats

It works. Sort of. But you know how goldfish have a thirty-second memory? My dog is the same.

This is what actually happens:

Tink is not impressed when, for the second day running, I fly through the air like a superhero on the end of Watson's lead. Neither are Chuck and Butch.

Positive Reinforcement clearly isn't working. We leave. I will have to devise another plan.

A *DOG'S LIFE*

Most film directors would shoot Tink's abduction scene on a studio set, where you can control things like daylight and the weather. But *ATTACK OF THE BLOBS!!!* is being directed by Tristram Valentino. Even among movie people (who are a pretty strange bunch) he's reckoned to be a bit of a nutter.

METHOD ACTING

Dustin Hoffman didn't sleep for three nights when he was filming *MARATHON MAN* because that's what happens to his character in the script. One of the other actors told him, "Try acting, it's much easier."

Although Tristram works in the fakest industry in the entire world, he likes to keep things "**real**". Ever heard of method actors? They're the guys who can't just pretend to cry or laugh on camera, they have to *feel* the emotion. They can do some pretty extreme stuff to get into character.

Well, Tristram Valentino is a method director – he wants real stunts in real locations. If he could employ real aliens to bite the heads off real New Yorkers, he'd do it.

REAL-LIFE HORROR

When filming the exploding chest scene in *ALIEN*, director Ridley Scott surprised the actors by showering them with real entrails from a nearby butcher's shop – so their screams were genuine.

He also likes to keep the action "**fresh**" and "**spontaneous**", which means that although the theme park is closed to the general public during filming, all the rides are still up and running because Tristram wants the mood and atmosphere to be right for the background action.

So me and Watson get to try everything out and we don't even have to queue!

We spend the rest of the afternoon:

| Paddling through the Amazon | Riding the Wild West rollercoaster | Flying on dragons in the Land of Legend |

The dragons are awesome! They're fixed to the floor on great big springs, so if you lean backwards and forwards you can make them soar and dive. And – get this! – a moving landscape is projected onto the walls so it feels like you're really flying.

But the City of Sensational Supers is my favourite. I drive the Batmobile through Gotham. I run up a skyscraper like Spider-Man. (OK, the wall is on the floor and the upright bit is actually a mirror and the whole thing is an optical illusion, but hey, it feels real!) I even get strapped into a harness and fly like Superman.

Day 1 has been brilliant, and I've got weeks and weeks of this! I wonder if life can get any better. I'm thinking not, but it turns out I'm wrong.

The cast and crew are still hard at it on Route 66 as Watson and I happily skip along to Tarzan's Tearooms. Then suddenly we hear this:

Who's that boy?

Stop him! Grab him!

Bring him here. And the dog. Yes, of course, naturally the dog.

Before we know what's happening, me and my pack brother are being seized by a couple of burly sparks and frogmarched to where the director is sitting.

Uh-oh. What have we done?

But it's OK, we're not in trouble. It's just
that Tristram Valentino is still on his fresh and
spontaneous kick. He thinks Watson and I look
"Ecstatic. Like the angels before the Fall." I have no
idea what he means, but it seems to be A Very Good
Thing. He wants us to be in his film – as part of the
crowd at the parade where Galaxion swoops down
and kidnaps Lucy-May. "You'll just have to stand
there, kid. The perfect picture of sweet innocence
before catastrophe strikes! You'll have them weeping
in the aisles."

I don't say anything. I don't have to. The producer,
Zoe Schwarz, escorts me to Dad's make-up trailer
with a note and a permission slip.

Dad's reaction is a bit weird.

To begin with, he is speechless. He does a goldfish impression, mouth opening and closing with no sound coming out. Then he finally finds his voice.

Is this some sort of joke? Does Tristram know what he's letting himself in for?

Zoe assures him it's not a joke.

Dad mutters what sounds suspiciously like "It's his funeral", and when Zoe says that I'll be getting paid, he starts laughing like a maniac. (I have no idea why.)

Finally he signs the form with a massive flourish.

DAD
- - - - - - - - - - - - -

I can hardly believe it!

Me and my dog are going to be movie stars!!!

DEAD END BG EPS

The next morning I have to get up at stupid o'clock with the rest of the cast and crew and stand in line to be made up along with the extras. Normally I hate early starts, but today I am mega excited.

We could get used to living life Hollywood-style.

Jacuzzi   Private limo   Private jet   Adoring fans

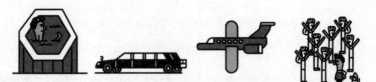

Tristram Valentino must be pretty gifted to have spotted my superstar quality. Right now he just wants me in the crowd, but who knows what he'll ask me

to do next? Me and Watson could be Captain Quark's sidekicks. We'd look great in capes!

In Make-up I'm expecting Dad

EXTRA EXTRAS

GHANDI had the most extras in movie history, with about 300,000 used in the film's big funeral scene.

to give me the full Tinkerbelle Cherry treatment –
sponges, brushes, the works. But all he does is dab
me with a bit of powder before telling me to BEHAVE
MYSELF AND KEEP MY DOG UNDER CONTROL
AT ALL TIMES. Then he sends me and Watson on
our way.

We head down to Route 66, where the extras are
all discussing Felicia and George. Eurgh!!!

When everything's finally in place, Tink emerges from her own personal trailer (all right for some!) and everyone gets into position for the first take.

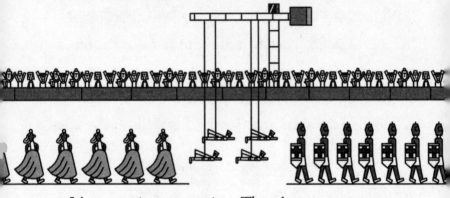

It's a massive procession. There's everyone from the Land of Legend – King Arthur, Lancelot, Guinevere, about a hundred and fifty knights in shining armour and an animatronic dragon. Then come the superheroes, suspended from wires on a moving crane so it looks like they're flying. Further on down the line are the Fairytale Fantasy characters: Cinderella and Snow White, Rapunzel and Sleeping Beauty, with matching princes posing beside them. A few hundred extras lining the route make it look like there's a real crowd of tourists watching the parade.

On screen, the finished scene will look like this:

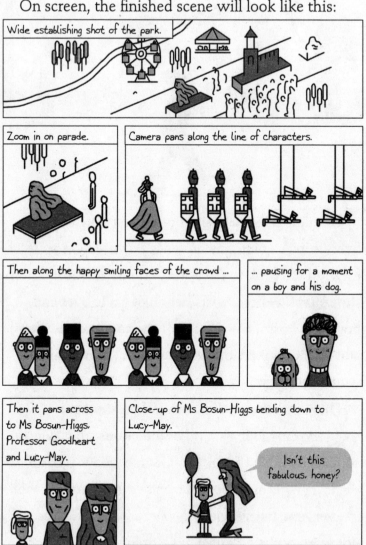

Wide establishing shot of the park.

Zoom in on parade.

Camera pans along the line of characters.

Then along the happy smiling faces of the crowd ...

... pausing for a moment on a boy and his dog.

Then it pans across to Ms Bosun-Higgs, Professor Goodheart and Lucy-May.

Close-up of Ms Bosun-Higgs bending down to Lucy-May.

Isn't this fabulous, honey?

PARP!

Tristram calls "**Action!**" and the first take begins. Everything's going fine until Ms Bosun-Higgs steps forward to speak to Lucy-May … and the heel of her shoe snaps. Felicia twists her ankle, falls over and – horror of horrors! – in front of the cast and the crew and all those gazillion extras, she expels a small but very audible fart.

There's a moment's silence. Then someone sniggers. Sniggering's kind of infectious, so it quickly spreads through the crowd. George (aka Galaxion) emits a giggle and soon everyone's laughing out loud.

Everyone but Felicia, who exudes pure fury as she points an accusing finger at George – who's dangling in his harness ready to swoop – and swears at him. Then she stalks off set, slamming her trailer door behind her.

The rest of us have to just stand there until she comes back. Tink stays with me and Watson and we play Kick the Frog,* which helps the time pass, but it takes Zoe nearly an hour to talk Felicia back out. When she finally succeeds, Felicia emerges, red-eyed, her mascara wrecked.

While Dad redoes her make-up, the production guys and sparks rush around getting everything reset. One of them picks something off the ground and Tink elbows me sharply in the ribs. "Look!" she whispers.

Crew 1:	What's that, Sid?
Crew 2:	The heel of her shoe.
Crew 1:	Snapped off?
Crew 2:	Looks more like it was cut through!
Crew 1:	Really? Have we got ourselves a Joker in the crew?

---

* It's not a real frog, obviously. It's a squeaky toy.

WILD WILD WEST (FFF)

Tink raises her eyebrows and stares at me but I have no idea why. I'm thinking: a Joker?* Wow! For the next five minutes I'm buzzing with possibilities.

Maybe the Joker will put a shark in the Amazonian Canoe Ride. Me and Watson could zap it with shark-repellent spray.

He might plant a bomb! And we'd have to go running through Moviewonderland looking for somewhere to get rid of it. But we'd win in the end, after a massive fight. *Kerpow!*

BEST BATMAN EVER

BATMAN: THE MOVIE was released in 1966. The Dynamic Duo battle four super-villains – the Penguin, the Joker, Catwoman and the Riddler – after the baddies capture the super dehydrator, a machine that reduces people to piles of multicoloured crystals.

---

* This is just like BATMAN: THE MOVIE, when the Joker tries to take over the world.

Then I snap back to the present and we get on with the long, slow business of filming. Tristram's decided that the camera has to zoom in for an extreme close-up of me. I have to stand there looking ecstatic. "You're delighted by the parade, kid. You can manage that, can't you? Imagine it's Christmas morning and Santa's just come down the chimney."

It sounds easy enough, but this acting stuff is harder than it looks.

I try giving my biggest and brightest smile, but Tristram yells, "Cut! Cut! Don't overdo it. You're supposed to be looking happy, not like you're having some kind of seizure."

THE 12 FACES OF
SAM

1 Happy   2 Sad

3 Scared   4 Bored

5 Nervous   6 Tired

7 Sweetly innocent   8 Guilty

9 Horrified   10 Embarrassed

11 Excited   12 Ecstatic

Tink whispers, "Stop twying so hard. Welax, Tham. Welax!" But it's not easy to welax when you've got a camera shoved up your nose. We do about sixty million takes and Tristram doesn't seem to be happy with any of them.

By lunchtime, my face is aching with the effort. Luckily child actors don't have to work a full day, so when our time's up, me and Tink are free to go. *Pher-ew!!*

We drift back towards King Arthur's Castle and Tink can't stop going on about Felicia and George. She's obsessed with their "twagically doomed womance". Typical girl.

Tink: I wonder why she dumped him?

```
Me:    [Yawning.] She said he
       dumped her.
Tink:  What? When?!
Me:    I saw her with Rhys. The
       first morning we were here.
Tink:  With Weese?
Me:    Yep. Mind you, the day
       before I thought I heard
       George say SHE dumped HIM.
Tink:  That's vewy strange...
```

Yeah, well, I think to myself, they don't come any stranger than movie actors – although I guess I'm one of them now.

But I'm not interested in grown-ups' bust-ups. I have my mind on more important things – like training my dog. Me and Tink say goodbye and I go off alone with my pack brother. We have work to do.

LETHAL WEAPON BG F

The dog-training books have failed me. Clearly the people who wrote them have never encountered a goldfish-brained Labrador. I need something more drastic, so I turn to the Internet. This is where I discover the Water Pistol Method.

This is a seriously cool training plan. It's like being in the Wild West.

It's supposed to work like this:

Owner has Bad Dog with Bad Habit.

Owner arms himself with weapon.

Owner lies in wait to catch Bad Dog indulging its Bad Habit.

GRR

Then, when it does...

KERPOW!

Bad Dog gets squirted with water.

If Bad Dog indulges Bad Habit again, it gets another squirt.

Bad Dog thinks:

Doing Bad Habit = Getting Water Blasted Between My Eyes.

Bad Habit stops!

This is brilliant! It doesn't hurt your dog, you don't have to yell and the dog doesn't even know it's you who's shooting the water!

This could work, I think to myself. It's the kind of ingenious approach that Sherlock Holmes would have approved of.

My to-do list for the rest of the day:

1) Buy water pistol

2) Become crack shot

After a visit to the Moviewonderland shop I am armed and dangerous. I'm now equipped with:

1) Water Sloosher
2) Aqua Blaster
3) Super Squirter

When I get Watson in the same room as Woopie, I want to be one hundred per cent sure I can zap him with the water. So for the rest of the afternoon, I engage in some serious shooting practice.

I'm getting good at this. Tomorrow afternoon I'll try it with Prince Rupert III.

Tomorrow, I will commence Operation Feline Peace.

FISH TANK

When Dad gets back from the day's shoot, he's dead impressed by my new training method. We head off to the Amazonian canoe ride so I can show him my new-found skills. Dad has a go with the Aqua Blaster and he's a pretty good shot, but we soon discover that animatronic parrots and water pistols don't mix.

After we're thrown off the ride, we join the cast and crew at the restaurant for dinner, and then most people drift off to the bar. Felicia sits in one corner

and George in the other. They're throwing evil looks
at each other because today's newspapers were full of
yet more stories about them.

HE TWO-TIMED ME!

She was dating some other guy!

**HE WAS SEEING OTHER WOMEN
BEHIND MY BACK!**

Dad, Watson and I are sitting in the George corner
happily discussing the merits of the Super Squirter
over the Water Sloosher, when I notice a funny smell.
Sort of fishy. And dead. Euw. I look around, and I
see that people are giving George strange looks and
edging away or finding other
people to talk to. He's wrinkling
up his nose and turning circles as
though he can't quite work out
where the pong is coming from.
He examines the bottom of his
shoe and shakes his head.

People and dogs have very different ideas about smells. There are all kinds of things that I find disgusting but Watson finds completely irresistible.

Rotting meat?
Delicious!

Mouldy cheese?
Mouth-watering!!

Horse manure?
Gourmet food!!!

So my dog is the only living creature in the bar who doesn't back away when George starts to stink. In fact, he decides the actor is his new best friend. My existence is completely forgotten. He sits in front of George trying his best to look loyal and appealing.

I am a good and well-behaved dog and I can smell that there is something fantastically delicious concealed about your person and I will be your very best friend if only you will please-oh-please give me some?

Well, luckily George doesn't mind Watson giving him a very thorough sniffing and then sticking his nose in his pocket. To begin with he's quite amused. Then Watson decides George has hidden something that needs eating NOW! This is what happens:

Watson tries to force his entire body, head first, into the pocket of George's designer suit.

There's a loud ripping sound.

RIP!

Something falls out of the jacket lining.

Prawns???!!!

Watson eats the evidence.

The Joker has struck again!

EXTRAS (WTA)

The next morning I have to be up early for another day on set. They need me in the background for continuity, plus Tristram wants another go at getting the perfect shot of my happy smiling face. But I'll be able to put Operation Feline Peace into action after lunch, so I take my weapons with me.

Filming goes pretty well. There's a lot of quiet sniggering about Felicia's fart and the prawns in George's jacket. People are

CONTINUITY

This is making sure things stay the same from shot to shot. You only really notice it when it goes wrong – like in *DIE HARD* when Bruce Willis's vest magically changes from white to olive green.

whispering among themselves, but like I said, actors can't talk quietly, not even extras. Felicia and George can hear every word, so the tension between Captain Quark and Galaxion cranks up and up until it's crackling in the air like electricity. They seem to have passed through the sad-about-the-break-up phase and moved swiftly on to the hate-each-other's-guts stage. When the cameras roll and the evil baddie swoops down to snatch Lucy-May, Felicia and George give each other a gazillion-watt glare.

It's so powerful it practically melts the tarmac. Tristram is thrilled to bits and praises them both for their acting – although as far as I can see, the hatred is one hundred per cent genuine.

Mid-morning, the director calls a break. Everyone dashes off to Craft Services to grab a hot drink and a doughnut. Everyone, that is, but Tink, who retires to her trailer because she isn't allowed to eat normal food like normal people. She

Craft Services
On a movie set, these guys do the grab-it-and-run food.

Catering
These guys organize the hot, sit-down meals.

invites me and Watson along too, but I tell her Watson needs a bit of a walk and sneak off to the van to stuff my face with three doughnuts (tasty) and

something called a Hershey bar (DISGUSTING). They call this chocolate? Americans have weird taste buds!

After the break, Tristram wants to try for my ecstatic close-up. I'm ready with my grin. We're all in position and Cameras One and Two are fine, but there's some kind of problem with Camera Three. It takes ages to get sorted and I start thinking about this afternoon's dog-training session.

I decide to spend some time practising with the Aqua Blaster in one hand and the Super Squirter in the other. I do that crossed hands thing as I fire both weapons at the same time!

I'm getting pretty good – I can now hit things from a distance of ten metres – when this happens:

PABOOM!!!!!

PABOOM!!!!!!

Oops!

The sparks react like this:

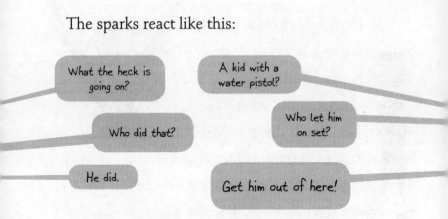

What the heck is going on?

A kid with a water pistol?

Who did that?

Who let him on set?

He did.

Get him out of here!

That is SO unfair! How was I supposed to know that light bulbs explode when you shoot them with water?

I expect to get fired on the spot, but I'm not. It turns out that while I was standing there, looking at the glass flying through the air with my mouth hanging open, Cameras One and Two were rolling. Tristram is one delighted director: he's finally managed to capture me looking genuinely ecstatic.

THE CAT'S MEOW

Once we're through with shooting for the day, me and Watson go back to the Guinevere Suite with Tink.

I've explained about the Water Pistol Method and Tink's well up for trying it out. I'm actually feeling a bit nervous because if this doesn't work I'm out of ideas.

Tink's mum and bodyguards, plus Donna and Trudi, all go into the other room, probably to gossip endlessly about George and Felicia, leaving us alone with Woopie and Watson.

The training session goes pretty well.

Watson is too busy scratching to notice Woopie at first, so Tink starts talking about the incident yesterday with Felicia's shoe. She doesn't know about what happened to George yet.

"Thomeone awound here has a vewy nasty thense of humour. I wonder who cut Felicia's heel?"

Someone who likes practical jokes. And guess what – whoever it is, he struck again last night in the bar! George's jacket was stuffed with prawns!

Prawns?

"Yep," I tell her. "Hidden in his suit so he wouldn't know they were there until they started to go off."

"I heard that Watson attacked him."

"He did not!" I say, leaping to the defence of my dog at the very same moment as he spots Tink's cat.

Oh yes! I am a crack shot. I would have been an ace gunslinger in the Wild West. I get Watson right between the eyes.

Watson shakes off the water, but then his goldfish brain takes over.

Another squirt. Another shake of the head.

In total, it takes the entire water reserves of:

the Water Sloosher   the Aqua Blaster   and most of
                                                      the Super Squirter

before Watson begins to realize:

Greeting + funny-looking dog = squirty water
???????????!!!!!!!!!!!!!!!

The carpet is sopping wet by the time he finally
gets it. Watson now decides there's something dodgy
about Prince Rupert III, so he sticks to my legs like
glue for the rest of the afternoon – which is a long
one because Tink decides we're due some quality
time with Barbie and Ken. While I'm trying to
persuade Tink that they should have a gunfight at the
OK Coral (and not a disco makeover), I'm keeping an
eye on the cat/dog situation.

Dad should have set me a project: *Using Watson
and Prince Rupert III as a case study, define the differences
between felines and canines.* By teatime I'm an expert.

When we eventually leave, Tink says, "I knew Woopie and Watson would be all wight in the end."

Personally, I'm not so sure. I've always thought Tink has a trace of the feline in her DNA, but now I reckon she has a bit of Labrador, too: she's certainly caught

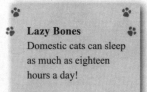

Lazy Bones
Domestic cats can sleep as much as eighteen hours a day!

Watson's Relentless Optimism. As I pull the door closed behind me, I notice Prince Rupert III's clear blue eyes fixed unblinkingly on my dog.

I suspect the THING is planning something.

THE *LOVE BUG* (FFF)

The remainder of the Moviewonderland shoot goes more or less smoothly. Galaxion does some swooping and Lucy-May gets snatched. Ms Bosun-Higgs transforms into Captain Quark and flies off after them. As for me and Watson – Ecstatic Boy and Dog – we just have to stand around until the part where Galaxion starts beheading people with his laser-beam eyes.

That's when Tristram Valentino suddenly decides that Watson and I should be the first to die.

An innocent child and his pet, slaughtered! Why, yes, of course! I am a genius!

Everyone's enthusiastic about the idea of me getting zapped, especially the sparks. You'd have thought they'd be annoyed, as Zoe has to rearrange the schedule and it means of load of extra work for them as well as for Wardrobe and Make-up, but they can't wait to see me die.

Watson and I get rigged up with Dad's special-effects squirty blood system.* I've got a massive bag

---

* To make a simple version, see the APPENDIX at the back.

SWEET MISERY

In *PSYCHO*, Alfred Hitchcock used chocolate syrup as fake blood.

of red liquid strapped around my middle and a zillion pipes leading up to my neck. Watson has the same, all disguised under layers of fake fur. I'm so excited! I plan to give an Oscar-winning performance.

My instructions are quite specific. When the director yells "**Action!**" I have to count to three, then work the hand pumps so the stage blood spurts everywhere as me and Watson hurl ourselves to the ground. I'm having so much fun that Tristram manages to get a few more ecstatic shots before my head comes flying off.*

---

* It doesn't really, obviously. The special-effects geeks will do that bit with CGI later on.

The first take goes well – but Tristram, being Tristram, decides he wants to do a second one. Which means all the blood has to be mopped up and everyone has to get changed into clean clothes and have their hair and make-up redone.

No worries – I'm having a great time, even though Tink keeps banging on about Felicia and George, wondering why they split up. It seems pretty obvious to me. They hate each other, end of story. Anyway, who cares? They're supposed to be arch-enemies so it won't do the film any harm. Tristram certainly isn't bothered. In fact, while the crew are mopping up the stage blood, he makes the most of the seething emotions whirling in the skies above Moviewonderland* by shooting some more close-ups of the filthy looks passing between Captain Quark and Galaxion.

So, filming's going brilliantly. The only time the friction between the two leads is a problem is in the

MONSTROUS MOVIE

In the 1954 film GODZILLA, the special effects involved an actor in a monster suit rampaging over miniature sets.

---

* Just like they do over Spook Central in GHOSTBUSTERS!

evenings when everyone's off duty. When George and Felicia are both in the restaurant you could cut the tension with a knife.

It gets even worse when Felicia starts looking at Rhys like this:

The Professor Goodheart actor offered her a shoulder to cry on and now she's flirting with him big time. It's enough to put anyone off their mega burger.

Meanwhile, George is stomping around with a big black cloud hanging over him, like a genuine supervillain. The paparazzi are having a field day.

Romance is in the air!

BEHIND-THE-SCENES SENSATION!

NEW LOVE BECKONS!

Dad says the off-screen drama is great for the movie because it brings loads of publicity, which will pretty much guarantee a big box office when it finally opens. "Audiences will love it, Sam. This movie is going to be a real winner. Roll on the Oscars!"

I couldn't agree more. I mean, there's that Best Supporting Actor category to think of. Who wouldn't award that to a slaughtered child and his mutilated pet?

TRANSFORMERS

Eventually we come to the last day of the
Moviewonderland shoot. Tomorrow morning we're
off to start working on the New York scenes.

Since I trained my dog to behave around cats,
Tink and I have got into a routine. We do the
filming in the morning and in the afternoon we
explore Moviewonderland. Naturally enough, Prince
Rupert III comes too – carried by Chuck and Butch
in his pink sparkly travelling box – although he
doesn't seem to like this very much. Two fully grown
bodyguards wrestling one small kitten into his crate is
quite a sight.

First Butch gets scratched to ribbons.

Then Chuck.

It takes them half an hour to cram him in.

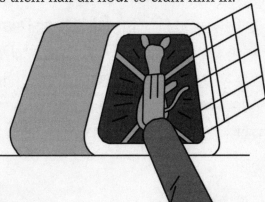

FILM FIRST

Walt Disney's first full-length animated feature film was *SNOW WHITE AND THE SEVEN DWARVES*, which came out in 1937. There were no computers back then, so every frame was hand drawn.

By now, we have tried out everything in the theme park. Well ... almost everything. I have managed to avoid the Fairytale Fantasy area so far, but today is Tink's last chance to see it and she inthists that we go there. When I'm reluctant, she says, eyes narrowing, "You wemember when Watson attacked Woopie?"

"Erm ... yes..."

"You thaid you'd do anything to make it up to me. You pwomised!"

I don't really have much choice but to agree. Come on, Sam, I tell myself. It can't be that bad, can it?

It can.

Tink's idea of a thrilling afternoon is soooooo different from mine. And Fairytale Fantasy is SOOOOOO lame! Desmond the Flying Dormouse never actually gets airborne, Little Bunny's Daring Journey is anything but daring and Pinkety-Boo's Scary Adventure definitely doesn't do what it says on the tin.

As for the Fairy Godmother's Palace? That is a total, genuine NIGHTMARE. It promises to "transform every raggedy Cinderella into a fairytale princess". And when the fairytale princess is fit for the ball, they take a gazillion souvenir photos.

Tink isn't exactly a raggedy Cinderella and you'd think she would have had enough of getting dressed up. It's her job! But no – she wants us to go in.

Uh-oh. Here comes Payback. Tink looks at me sideways and says innocently:

You know, Watson could have killed poor little Woopie! But I forgive you because you're my vewy best fwend. Shall we go into the Faiwy Godmother's Palace?

This is blackmail. But what can I do? So I spend the afternoon being preened and primped alongside Tink. So does Watson, who is not at all keen on being my cute animal sidekick. We are:

Cinderella and Prince Charming

(and mouse)

Snow White and Prince Handsome

(and bluebird)

Sleeping Beauty
and
Prince Rich

(and squirrel)

Tink is in heaven, but I have never felt so
humiliated in my life. Fortunately, my pack brother,
the best and most wonderfully gifted and intelligent
dog in the universe, finally comes to the rescue.
We are about to be made into the Little Mermaid
and Prince Wonderful when he decides his lobster
costume is edible.

It's not, of course, but by the time he discovers the
truth, he's pulled out most of the stuffing. The Fairy
Godmother is not pleased, and we get swiftly hustled
out of the palace. Biggest relief EVER!!

I've had enough of Moviewonderland. Boy am
I looking forward to New York.

NEW YORK, NEW YORK

*"New York, New York. So good they named it twice."** The
words of the old song Dad hums all the way there are
true. This place is AMAZING.

Tink flies there in her own private jet but the rest
of us get on planes that Cosmic Films have chartered
for the cast and crew. Because it's just us, normal
aeroplane rules are relaxed and Watson is allowed to
ride in the cabin instead of being squashed into a sky
kennel and put in the hold.

---

* Although they actually called it New Amsterdam to begin with.

We fly from one side of America all the way to the other and it takes almost six hours. Big country or what? But we're crossing time zones

again so we actually land nearly nine hours after we set off.

We come in low, right over the Statue of Liberty. I get a Captain Quark's-eye view of the Empire State Building and Manhattan and pretty much the whole of the city before we land at JFK airport.

JFK airport is named after John Fitzgerald Kennedy, the 35th President of the USA, who was assassinated in 1963.

A line of yellow taxis awaits us. Me, Watson and Dad climb into one and we're driven through the

The total area of the
USA is 9,826,629
kilometres. That's
more than twice the
size of the European
Union, but only half
the size of Russia and
three tenths of the size
of Africa.

mean streets of New York. I've seen so many movies based here that it's all uncannily familiar, like being on a massive set. I'm expecting Spider-Man to swing down from a skyscraper, Iron Man to fly past or the Teenage Mutant Ninja Turtles to come bursting out of the sewers.

Everyone is staying in the Olde Countree Hotel, which overlooks Central Park. Tink gets the Penthouse Suite, of course, but our room is pretty good too. OK, the décor's a bit weird (Scottish theme – not sure why!), but it has a bath so big you can swim in it, free Wi-Fi and a massive TV that has satellite and cable, so I can watch any channel I could ever wish for.

The first thing me and Dad do is take Watson for a walk in Central Park. I'm half expecting everyone to burst into song like they do in *ENCHANTED*. It's here that my pack brother discovers the joys of:

1) Snatching basketballs and running off with them.

You'd think those guys would be impressed by his super-athletic sprinting but they were seriously annoyed!

2) Barking at street entertainers.

It wasn't Watson's fault he put that man off his acrobatics. He needed more focus, man!

3) Marking his territory on living statues.

The man had been standing perfectly still, how was Watson supposed to know he wasn't made of stone...?!

Dad's beginning to look seriously stressed, but all the shouting and yelling doesn't dampen my dog's enthusiasm. He's just found some bins stuffed with hot-dog wrappers. Paradise!

Then we come to a lake filled with ducks and Watson plunges head first into the water. He sincerely thinks he can catch up with them.

Not a chance, buddy. OK, you can swim, but I can fly.

Watson loves New York. As far as he is concerned, life does not get any better than this. I think I agree.

THE *FLOWER* OF EVIL (BG) (WTA)

We are eating our tea in the Olde Countree Hotel with the rest of the cast and crew. Tristram is talking to Barry, the stunt co-ordinator, about something technical. Barry looks a bit anxious. George is nowhere to be seen, but Felicia is sitting in the far corner with Rhys, chomping on a teeny tiny bowl of salad.

Then this arrives for her:

A dozen red roses. Even I know that's supposed to be romantic.

Felicia looks a bit puzzled and pulls out the card that's stuck to the cellophane. When she reads what's written on it her face splits into a grin.

She gets up from the table without another word to Rhys and heads towards the door, eyes scanning the room as if she's looking for someone. Then halfway across the restaurant she lets out an ear-splitting scream.

YEEEAAAAAAAAAAACCCCKKKKK!!!!!

JOKER

Film director Alfred Hitchcock loved playing practical jokes, often putting whoopee cushions on his dinner guests' chairs.

Felicia's shriek is so loud it shatters every glass in the place. (Well, it doesn't *actually*, but it does make one or two waiters drop their trays and every diner in the room spill their drink.)

And the reason? There are things in the roses. *Living* things. *Slimy* living things. Which are now slithering up Felicia's arms and into her clothes…

Euw! The bouquet is stuffed with slugs! It looks like the Joker has followed us to New York!!

Horrified, Felicia drops the flowers and runs from the room. Rhys follows in hot pursuit, frantically trying to brush the slugs off her. The place erupts as everyone starts talking at once.

Meanwhile, Watson spots a square of white card lying on the carpet beside the flowers. Squelching through the slugs, he dashes to retrieve it, thinking:

Fetch! + Sam = FOOD!

He drops it in my lap, then sits, expecting a treat, so I give him a bit of burger before I examine what he's brought me.

It's the card that came with the bouquet.

Please accept this gift. I am sending what you deserve.

George xxx

My razor-sharp Sherlock brain swings into operation.

Q: Who sent the slug-filled flowers?
A: George

Q: Does that mean George is the Joker?
A: Yes... Maybe.

Q: Did George also cut the heel off Felicia's shoe?
A: Probably.

Q: But if George is the Joker, who put the prawns in his jacket?
A: Erm ... no idea.

I need to find out if George really is the Joker. I reckon I'll have to poke around a bit on set. I check Dad's call sheet for tomorrow.

The first New York location is the Statue of Liberty, where Tristram will shoot the epic climax. I read the script before we flew to America, so I know how the final cut will look.

COSMIC FILMS
Spacex Studios · 1823 Galaxy Drive · Moontown · CA 932

ATTACK OF THE BLOBS!!!

Call sheet: 31

Monday 6 September
Cars and ferry to transport cast and crew to location

DIRECTOR	Tristram Valentino
PRODUCER	Zoe Schwarz
1st AD	Eric Griffin
UNIT BASE	Vessels moored at Liberty Island
LOCATION MANAGER	Carole Mann
STUNT CO-ORDINATOR	Barry Lasseter

SET/SYNOPSIS Scene 127

Galaxion flies down...

ATTACK OF THE BLOBS!!!

Galaxion lands on the Statue of Liberty with the abducted Lucy-May.

He tosses the little girl high in the air.

She plummets to earth …

… but hits the flame of the statue's torch as she falls …

… and is left clinging to the iron railings that surround the flame.

Professor Goodheart looks on helplessly.

Captain Quark flies down and tries to save Lucy-May.

Captain Quark gets zapped and falls from the sky …

… plunging into the ocean.

Galaxion flies down to Lady Liberty's feet. His radioactive power passes up through the statue.

Laser beams shoot out from her eyes ...

... and her torch becomes a real flame.

The torch sends a beam into the sky, ripping apart the skin that separates one galaxy from another.

A wormhole is opened and alien blob monsters begin to pour through. It's an invasion!!!

The aliens land on Liberty Island and squirt toxic slime ...

... then they bite the heads off every tourist in the place.

The aliens move on to the rest of New York City just as Captain Quark surfaces and flies across Liberty Island to rescue Lucy-May.

Any other director would settle for using computer wizardry and scale models to create these scenes, but this is Tristram Valentino. He's employed an army of stunt guys who will be poised and ready for action as soon as Dad transforms them ...

from this: to this:

Tristram might like to keep things real, but not even a stunt co-ordinator as talented as Barry Lasseter can arrange for actual alien blob monsters to fall from the actual sky. However, what he's planned comes pretty close.

The wormhole sequence will be filmed in three sections:

HOW IT WILL LOOK ⟶ **HOW IT WILL BE FILMED**

The wormhole opens.

The wormhole bit is all done with CGI.

Blob monsters cascade through the sky ...

Stunt people are dropped from planes. The freefall is filmed and cut just before their parachutes open.

... and land on the ground.

Other stunt people whizz down zip wires rigged from cranes near the statue's head.

When the sections are spliced together, the blob monsters will look like they've zoomed right out of the wormhole all the way down to the earth.

The third part of the shot – the one with all the cranes and wires – will actually be filmed first.

I know my character got zapped in Moviewonderland, but I'm kind of hoping Tristram will offer me a second part as one of the aliens. I'd love to have a go at whizzing down those wires.

As we pass Tristram in the corridor of the Olde Countree Hotel later that evening I try my best to look like a blob monster. I'm hoping I'll get noticed again, and when he stops, I think, Yay! Result!

But all he says to Dad is, "Gee, is your kid OK, Marcus? It looks like he needs a doctor!"

ZIPPING AROUND

In *IRON MAN 3*, the crew had to put up a whole mile of zip line for one stunt sequence.

LIBERTY STANDS STILL BG WTA

As part of my cunning undercover investigation I persuade Dad that it would be Highly Educational for me to see the Statue of Liberty up close. He agrees and says he'll take me along for the first day's shooting. Yes! Unfortunately he sets me a great long worksheet. It has 50 questions!*

Statue of Liberty worksheet

1. Which country gave the statue to America?
_____

2. In what year was it given? _____

3. What is Lady Liberty's shoe size? _____

4. How large is her waist? _____

5. Who designed the statue? _____

6. Who designed the internal support structure that holds her up, and what other landmark was he famous for designing? _____

5. Write down the poem that is written at the feet of the statue. _____
_____
_____
_____

6. Who was the poem written by? _____

7. Draw a picture of the statue over the page.

page 1/20

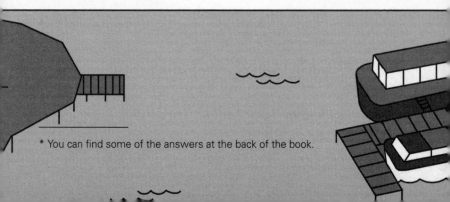

* You can find some of the answers at the back of the book.

As far as Dad's concerned, that covers English, Geography, History and Art.

In the morning, Dad, Watson and I take the ferry over to Liberty Island. The place is going to be full of plummeting aliens and screaming extras being zapped and eaten, so Cosmic Films can't have their base on land. Instead, they've hired a fleet of yachts and barges and other boats that are moored all along the jetty. Basically, they've created a floating town. It's well impressive.

Dad sets to work as soon as we arrive. Tink gets whizzed out on a speedboat and goes straight into Make-up. Then she and her entire entourage (including Prince Rupert III) are installed in the most luxurious of the luxury yachts to wait until Tristram Valentino is ready for them.

> The Statue of Liberty is 46.03 m from base to torch. Her nose is 1.37 m long.

Meanwhile, me and Watson have a good look around Lady Liberty. I answer some of the questions on my worksheet, then we climb the 354 stairs to her crown. The view is awesome but I have the knees of an Old Age Pensioner by the time I've gone up and down. My legs can hardly hold me up and Watson's tongue is hanging out so far it's practically scraping the ground.

Investigating George will have to wait: I need some serious chilling out time. I head for the ferry back to the mainland, but Tink spots me and I am summoned to her yacht.

There's some sort of hitch with the wires on Tink's harness, so she hasn't actually done anything all morning and she's mega bored. This means me and Watson get to lounge around on a boat that looks like this:

That's fine by me! My knees are so jelly-like from the climb, it's a relief to relax in style. Tink decides Barbie and Ken should be superheroes, so I fashion a collection of pink blob monsters out of the Silly Putty that Cosmic Films have so thoughtfully provided in Tink's games and toys cupboard.

We're both having great fun hurling blob monsters around the room when Tink says, "I heard about the slugs in Felicia's flowers. Was it another pwactical joke, do you think?"

I start to tell her about the note that came with the bouquet when disaster strikes.

Watson is asleep on his back with his legs in the air. He barely noticed Prince Rupert III when we arrived – the training worked! Prince Rupert III, meanwhile, retreated to a place of safety (Chuck's head). Now he suddenly stalks up to me and rubs his face against my legs, purring as if he's actually pleased to see me. He even starts rolling around on the floor on his back.

If Watson does this, it means he wants his tummy tickled. Instinctively, I reach down to stroke Woopie.

Then I discover another of the many differences between dogs and cats:

PET-STROKING GUIDE

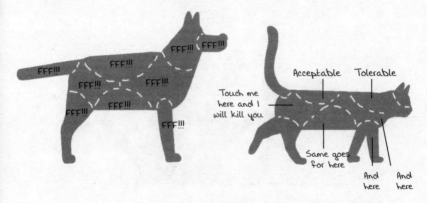

When my fingers make contact with the kitten's fur, he does this:

Aaaargh! He thinks my hand is a bunny he must disembowel! I can't shake him off!

I shriek. Watson wakes. Stands up. Prince Rupert III lets go of me and decides to launch an attack on the Filthy Canine instead. He springs across the floor in two great bounds and swipes Watson across the nose.

Watson yelps.

"Poor Woopie!" says Tink. "Did the nasty doggy scare you?"

WHAT???!!! Worse is to come. Woopie begins to hiss and spit.

MEEYEOWLHISSTLESPLITZ!!!!!

Watson, keeping his eyes firmly fixed on the funny-looking-dog-who-causes-water-to-squirt-mysteriously-from-nowhere, starts backing nervously into the corner.

"Woopie!" calls Tink. "Come here!"

But Woopie is a Feline Ninja. He can sense that victory is in his grasp. He advances on my dog, stands up on his back legs and raises his front legs so they look like arms.

Then ... SNIKT!!!

His claws flick out like Wolverine's.

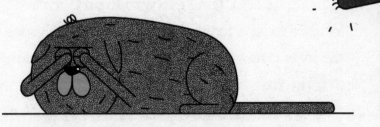

I hurl myself across the room to save my pack brother. Tink orders, "Chuck, do thomething!"

And Chuck does. He intercepts the Leaping Ninja, who lands, claws fully extended, on his well-muscled thigh. Chuck screams like a girl, but he has prevented a full-scale assault on my dog – although pwecious little Woopiekins has still managed to give poor Watson a bloody nose.

Criminal Animals
Mexican police jailed a donkey in 2008 after it bit and kicked two men. In 2013, the Egyptian authorities detained a stork on suspicion of spying. (It had been tagged by scientists tracking its migration.)

I am super cross, especially when Tink blames Watson. She says my dog must have done something to her kitten – looked at him funny, maybe. "He wouldn't attack for no weason!"

She is wrong. Wrong, wrong, wrong.

In a state of extreme **glowerment**, me and Watson go back to the Old Countree. Investigating the Joker is now officially at the bottom of my to-do list. There is something more important at the top.

That cat is a criminal! He must be stopped. Next time I come to Liberty Island I am bringing my water pistols.

Tomorrow, while Tink is occupied on set, I plan to train her cat.

SECRET AGENT (FFF)

At 5 a.m. the following morning, Dad is bumbling around in the dark trying not to wake me as he gets ready for work. As soon as he leaves, I'm ready for action. He has left me another note.

STAY HERE AND DO ALL
THE WORK YOU DIDN'T
DO WHEN WE WERE AT
MOVIEWONDERLAND!

He's dumped a truckload of books and worksheets on my bedside table. I am supposed to stay here in the hotel room all day with Watson and his bandaged nose.

But this is New York, New York! Home to the Ghostbusters, Men in Black and Spider-Man. Would any of them take this lying down? I think not.

Tink's cat's assault on my dog cannot go unpunished.

Today, Sam Swann will become …

THE CANINE AVENGER!!!!

Getting onto Liberty Island won't be a problem. Dad has this habit of emptying all the loose change from his trouser pockets into the drawer by his bed each night and forgetting to put it back in the morning, so I have a fistful of dollars for the fare. There will be so many extras milling around pretending to be genuine tourists that no one will pay attention to one more. The only problem is if Tink spots me. Or Dad. I'll need a disguise.

My thinking goes like this:

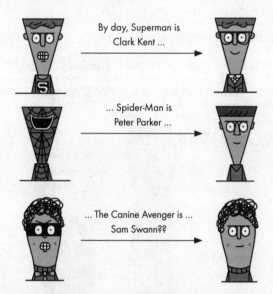

By day, Superman is Clark Kent ...

... Spider-Man is Peter Parker ...

... The Canine Avenger is ... Sam Swann??

No – what The Canine Avenger needs is a mild-mannered alter ego. And guess what – Dad's not the only make-up genius in the family.

I know where Dad keeps his secret stash of supplies. There are a few things in the room I can use too.

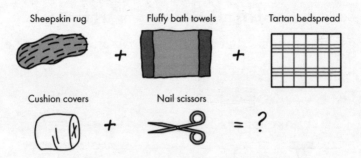

Sheepskin rug + Fluffy bath towels + Tartan bedspread

Cushion covers + Nail scissors = ?

I give the rug and towels a bit of a trim, then, with a few dollops of glue, it takes a mere forty-seven minutes to transform my pack brother and myself into this:

Cushion-cover hat

Beard and moustache from towel trimmings

Bedspread kilt and cape

Sheepskin trimmings to make Watson look like a Border collie

On set, Sam Swann and Watson would get noticed. But no one will pay any attention to Tavish McTavish, an elderly Scottish tourist, and his shaggy wee sheepdog, Hamish.

THE KARATE KID FFF

On the ferry, we secrete ourselves in the middle of the pack of extras. Once we reach Liberty Island, we hang back and then peel away, silently and speedily transforming from Tavish McTavish and his shaggy wee sheepdog into The Canine Avenger and his sidekick, Haggis.

It's still early. We lurk in the shadows until we see Tink and all her entourage going into Make-up. It's chaos on set, with everyone frantically getting ready for the day's shooting. Sparks and stunt guys are running in every direction, so no one notices me and Watson sneaking along the jetty.

We glide like shadows past Felicia's yacht.

Have you seen this headline? "FELICIA IS A WASTE OF SPACE, SAYS GEORGE." I could kill him!

Then George's.

Can you believe this? "GEORGE IS A LOSER, SAYS FELICIA." I hope she rots in hell!

At last we reach Tink's. We peer inside, where, as we expected, Prince Rupert III is sitting alone on his silk cushion.

We slide through the door and

close it carefully behind us. Woopie is not happy to see Watson. He prepares to launch another assault, and – SNIKT! – out come the claws.

But he's reckoned without The Canine Avenger. I'm like Bruce Willis in *Die Hard*. There's no stopping me. I dive, roll and … shoot!

SPLAT!!

The jet of water from the Super Squirter narrowly misses Watson and hits Woopie smack in his belly button.

Woopie freezes, stock-still, for about thirty seconds. He is clearly in shock. Then he gives himself a good shake and retires to his silk cushion.

My dog might think he's a Jedi Master but he's not the only deluded animal around here. Prince Rupert III now thinks Watson can squirt water out of his nose.

Mission accomplished!!!

> Liberty Island is one
> of the three Oyster
> Islands in New York
> harbour, where the
> Native Americans used
> to gather oysters.

The Canine Avenger and Haggis transform back into their mild-mannered alter egos and head for the ferry.

We walk right past Tristram but he doesn't even glance in our direction. He's just bumped into Rhys and they're high-fiving.

```
Tristram:    Hey, buddy! How's it
             going?
Rhys:        Like clockwork.
Tristram:    All set for the next
             stunt?
Rhys:        Oh yes.
```

KIDNAPPED (F)

My day's work is done. I'm at the hotel knee-deep in home-school work when Dad surprises me by coming back early. I expect him to be pleased, especially as I've finally cracked long division, but he doesn't even notice the mountain of sums I've climbed.

All he says is, "Bad news, Sam. Tink's kitten is missing."

For a moment I'm:

1. Horrified   2. Guilty   3. Nervous

Then he adds, "It's odd. She says he was there when we broke for coffee, and Chuck and Butch agree. When she went to find him at lunchtime, he'd gone."

Phew! For a second I thought maybe I'd left the cabin door open. I feel sorry for Tink, but at least it wasn't my fault Woopie got out. I wonder if the Joker has struck again…?

But I don't get any time to think about it because apparently Tink is inconsolable and Dad says it is my duty as her BFF* to comfort her. We need to get up to the penthouse right now.

"What if she cries on me?" I say, panicking.

Dad gives me a hard stare and drags me to the lift (sorry, elevator).

---

* Best Friend For ever.

As soon as we're inside Tink's suite, she flings her arms around my chest and squeezes me so hard I can hardly breathe. She's surprisingly strong for a small person. Then she's weeping and wailing.

Oh, Tham! What's happened to my poor little Woopiekins?

He probably ran away because you called him that, I think to myself, but I am far too tactful to say so. "Well," I announce, in my best Consulting Detective voice, "he's a clever sort of cat. I expect he'll turn up."

"Twistwam says he might have dwowned!!!"

Gee, thanks, Tristram. Thoughtful of you to say so. Not.

The film director has Tink's imagination working

overtime. All kinds of things are going through her head. Has her cat been:

Or is he the victim of a fiendish plot? Has he been:

The girl is in floods of tears. "I'll never see Woopie again!"

It's all dead awkward and I don't really know what to say, so I just keep patting her on the arm. Now I know how Rhys felt when Felicia cried all over him.

I whisper, "I tell you what, Tink. Me and Watson

will sneak on set tomorrow, OK? He's a sniffer dog
– I've been training him for ages. If anyone can find
Prince Rupert it's him."

Tink does one of her million-dollar-a-movie smiles.
But her lower lip wobbles when she says, "Would you,
Tham? I'd be vewy vewy gwateful."

"I'll find him for you, Tink," I tell her. "I promise."

THE *INCREDIBLES* (FFF)

For the second day running, Tavish McTavish and wee Hamish are going to ride the ferry to Liberty Island.

The hotel has given us fresh towels, so I'm OK for a moustache and beard. The trouble is, I've already trimmed most of the hair off the rug and they don't give you a fresh one of those every day. I don't have enough rug trimmings to go around Watson's middle. Instead, I take off a cushion cover and borrow one of Dad's belts and do this:

★ At least 11 Presidents
★ of the USA were of
★ Scottish descent.

Cushion cover   Scissors   Dad's belt   Wee Hamish costume!

 + 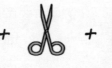 + =

DON'T TRY THIS AT HOME!

So far, so good! I decide to take the Aqua Blaster and the Super Squirter just in case. If we find Woopie, I don't want him attacking my dog again.

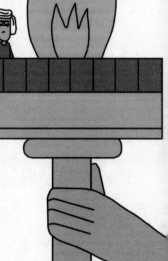

Today Tink has to film the bit where she's dangling off the Statue of Liberty's torch. She'll be attached to a safety harness, so there's no danger of her actually falling – but even so, it's got to be pretty scary. Any other actress would use a body double, but ages ago – before I met her – there was an accident on the set of GNOME IS WHERE THE HEART IS. Since then, Tink has sworn that she'll always do her own stunts.

Tinkerbelle Cherry may be a bit of a diva at times but she's

MILLION-DOLLAR STUNT

The costliest aerial stunt ever performed was in CLIFFHANGER. Stuntman Simon Crane crossed from one plane to another at a height of 4,500 m. It was so dangerous that the stunt was only performed once and he was paid $1,000,000 for it.

HIDDEN SUPERSTARS

Stunt men and women are just about the only people in Hollywood who don't have a category in the Oscars.

also a real professional. She might be really upset about her missing kitten, but I know she'll turn up on time and be ready to go the moment everything's set up.

By the time me and Watson – aka Tavish McTavish and wee Hamish – reach Liberty Island, Tink is already in position on the statue's torch. It's been closed to the public since 1916, but Tristram, being Tristram, has special permission to open it up for filming. At ground level, the gossip buzzing around the extras is that Tink's barely holding herself together.

Poor kid, she looked awful!

Did you see her eyes? So red!

She's heartbroken about that kitty.

Should she be working today at all?

They're not the only ones who are bothered. Barry Lasseter is looking really unhappy. The only person who doesn't seem to be concerned is Tristram Valentino.

Barry: Do we have to go ahead
            with this?

Tristram: Yes, we do.

Barry: But she's crying!

Tristram: Her character is
            supposed to be! So what
            if the tears are real?

I have gone right off Tristram. But he's not my problem right now. I have a job to do. Today, Tavish McTavish and Hamish become:

THE FELINE FINDER AND SNIFFEROO!!!

This is our very first Missing Persons case.* And
I have an idea. I remember how, before I got Watson,
Gran's next-door neighbour's tabby cat was always
getting itself shut in our shed. (After Watson arrived,
the cat didn't set foot in our garden again.) I wonder if
Woopie has got himself trapped on someone's yacht.

We lurk in the shadows until shooting begins,
then we start creeping along jetties and up and down
gangplanks, calling Woopie's name.

To begin with it's quite exciting. But as the
morning wears on and we don't find so much as a
single paw print, it becomes frustrating. The cast and
crew will break for coffee soon and I was hoping to
have found Woopie by then so I could cheer Tink up.

*   OK, missing cat,
    but you know
    what I mean.

I give my dog a stern talking-to. He's my sidekick, after all, and occasionally sidekicks are supposed

SIDEKICKS

Batman has Robin. Sherlock Holmes has Dr Watson. Hercule Poirot has Captain Hastings.

to come up with good ideas. I tell Watson this is his chance to prove himself as a sniffer dog.

I suddenly remember that Tink has given me the cushion that Woopie sleeps on. I let Watson sniff it, like they do in the movies, and Watson gets really excited. His nose goes down, his tail goes stiff. He looks like Napoleon in THE ARISTOCATS, or Dug in UP. I think he's on to something. He's off and I'm in hot pursuit…

He stops! Points!! Result!!!

But no. Watson is on the trail of … an apple core … a crust of bread … a sliver of orange peel … a wad of gum.

Useless animal!

I am about to give up when we both hear a faint meowing. We follow the sound, which is coming from a yacht near the end of the row. It gets louder and louder until it turns into a muffled but fully enraged:

MEEYEOWLHISSTLESPLITZ!!!!!

Watson is terrified. He whimpers and glues himself to my legs for protection, but I am an intrepid superhero.

Into the yacht we stride, through the lounge, towards the cabins. I try one door, then the other, when … KERBANG! Out bursts Woopie.

I don't know whose yacht it is, and quite honestly I don't care. What a brilliant surprise for Tink! I try to pluck the kitten off my head, but it's easier said than done: he's hooked his claws into me and I'm in danger of getting my ears pierced.

I've just about managed to prise him free when I hear the Thump! Thump! Thump! of feet on the gangplank and the sound of voices approaching. Two people have come onto the yacht. Weird. It's not coffee time yet.

I'm about to walk out and tell them what I'm doing here – I mean, I've found Tink's cat! I'll be the hero of the hour!!

Then I stop in my tracks.

She's not upset enough. I guess I'll have to drown the thing for real!

This is followed by the sound of someone laughing. And it's not a nice, heartwarming chuckle – it's more like the Joker's snigger in *SCOOBY-DOO MEETS BATMAN*.

So I hide in a cupboard* instead.

---

* Sorry, *closet*.

HEAR NO EVIL BG 3A

My pack brother and I are crouching in the closet. Prince Rupert III is pawing at us through the slats of the door.

In the other room, I can hear someone who sounds suspiciously like Tristram Valentino.

You've seen *Saboteur*, right?

No...

But *I've* seen it. My mind does this:

SABOTEUR PG

Spy thriller 1942 US BW 104 mins

Director: Alfred Hitchcock

Features a famous finale on the torch of the Statue of Liberty where the bad guy falls over the railings, then slides down until he's left clinging to the statue's thumb ... before plummeting to his death.

FILM FAKE!

The falling scene in
SABOTEUR was actually
filmed in a studio, with
the statue and the
ground added in later.

I happen to know that when
they filmed that scene, the
camera was jerked up and away
on a length of rope to make
the actor look like he was falling a long, long way.
But Tristram Valentino isn't that sort of director.
Tinkerbelle Cherry will be on the real Statue of
Liberty, dangling over real empty space, while
stuntmen dressed as alien blob monsters whizz past
her on zip wires.

Except Tink's only supposed to be hanging on to
the railings. Isn't she?

"I've made Barry rig her harness to give an extra
drop," says Tristram.

"He's OK with that?" asks the other guy, who
sounds like Rhys.

"If he wants to work in Hollywood again, he'll do
what I tell him. She'll slide right down the thumb."

"And she doesn't know about it?"

"Nope. She'll think she's really falling! I'll have a
camera rigged to get a real close shot of her face.

She'll be scared senseless! The sound crew had better make sure they get those screams on tape." That snigger again.

At this, my mind does a magnificent piece of deduction. Sherlock Holmes would be proud of me.

Joke 1
Heel sawn through.

End result?
Felicia hates George.

Joke 2
Prawns in suit.

End result?
George hates Felicia.

Joke 3
Slugs in bouquet.

End result?
They hate each other more than ever.

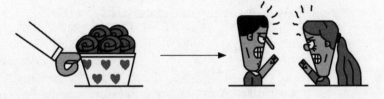

Which is all really good for the film.

And lastly…

Joke 4
Tink's cat disappears.

End result?
She's up there sobbing
her heart out.

Which is also really good for the film.

Q: Who cares most about the film?
A: The director.

Tristram Valentino? *He's* the Joker? He's the *Joker*?!
OMG! HE'S THE JOKER!
He's sitting in the next room! Rhys is his evil
henchman!! And I'm stuck in the closet!!!

Who knows what Tristram and Rhys will do if they find me. I'll have to stay hidden until they go.

Then I hear Tristram say, "I need more tears. It's time I threw that kitty-cat overboard." He comes into the cabin, crooning, "Here, kitty, kitty." But his soft, soothing voice changes the second his hands close around Woopie. "GOTCHA!"

Through the slatted closet doors, I see him take the kitten by the scruff of the neck, open the porthole and do this:

I thought that Tink's cat and
my dog were doomed to be arch-
enemies, but dogs have an instinct
when it comes to bad guys.
Watson bursts out of the closet like
an avenging hero, hackles raised,
teeth bared, snarling. I – The Feline
Finder – am right behind him.

Tristram whips round and stares at us, open-
mouthed. Which gives Prince Rupert III enough time
to sink his claws into the director's hand and clamber
up his arm back into the cabin.

The kitten scampers over to us. Now all we have
to do is escape.

Rhys is blocking the doorway.

"Catch that kid!"
Tristram yells as blood
drips from his hand.
"Get him. Now!!"

But I am armed and
dangerous.

Blam! I zap Rhys between the eyes with the Aqua Blaster. **BLAM!** I do the same to Tristram with the Super Squirter.

Then the three of us – dog, cat and boy – run for our lives, out of the cabin, through the yacht, down the gangplank and towards the Statue of Liberty.

I don't have a plan, but it seems that Woopie is determined to get to Tink. He takes the lead and runs towards the statue with Watson and me close behind. I don't know what's happened to Tristram, but Rhys is hot on our heels, yelling, "Stop! STOP!!"

We are playing chase!
Ohboyohboyohboy,
this is my
favourite game!

We duck and dive through the crowd of extras.
The belt comes off Watson's wee tartan coat and
Woopie gets entangled in a shopping bag.

We reach Lady Liberty and we're off up the stairs.
There's no stopping us.

To begin with, the chase is like this:

But by the hundredth stair we're more like this:

By the two hundredth we're like this:

By the time we head into Lady Liberty's right arm
(man, it's narrow in here!) we're practically on our
knees.

This last bit is more like a ladder than a staircase.
Woopie is springing from rung to rung like a mountain

goat, but Labradors aren't
the most agile of dogs. I'm having
to push and drag and carry my pack brother
every inch of the way, and Rhys is closing in. He's
dressed in his Professor Goodheart costume but
there's nothing goodhearted about the way he's
swearing and cursing us.

He's almost caught up when the three of us finally
emerge out onto the torch.

I guess the techies are all set and the actors are all
in position and Tristram doesn't have any choice but
press ahead with the take, because from far below
I hear a faint cry of "**Action!**" and then this happens:

Watson – thinking this is part of the game – springs over the barrier after Woopie.

I'm on the end of his lead, and I get jerked after him.

Me and Watson catch Tink's legs as they fly past.

... but the harness isn't designed to take the weight of two kids, 30 kilos of Labrador and a kitten...

The cable snaps. The four of us plummet towards the ground.

We hold on tight ...

Alien blob monsters are flashing past. One crashes into Tink and she grabs him.

Watson's lead loops itself over a zip wire ...

... and, like superheroes, we whizz safely down to earth.

THE *FINAL CURTAIN* BG F

We land on the grass slap-bang in the middle of
Liberty Island, the four of us squishing the poor
unfortunate blob monster underneath. Woopie gets
well and truly slimed. The producer looks stunned.
Barry Lasseter is white-faced and unable to speak –
all that's coming out of his mouth is a high-pitched
squeak. But the extras are all talking at once.

Then the sparks and the other techie guys start joining in:

People are laughing and exclaiming, until Barry Lasseter finally finds his voice. "Yeah, Tristram," he says coldly. "Why don't you tell us all what you're playing at?"

For the first time, Tristram Valentino doesn't have a clue what to say or do. He shrugs, goes red, then mutters something about being fresh and spontaneous.

I point an accusing finger at the director and say, "You catnapped Prince Rupert the Third!"

Tink looks at me, then at him, and demands, "Is this twue?"

Tristram goes even redder. "**shut up, kid,**" he mumbles desperately.

But I don't shut up. I tell Tink, "*And*, he was planning to drown him just to make you cry more!"

A gasp of horror ripples through the cast and crew. Catnapping is one thing. But attempted catricide?!*

You were going to hurt Woopie...?

He's the Joker!

---

* Killing a person is called homicide, killing a father is called patricide, killing a mother is matricide, killing a brother is fratricide and killing a sister is sororicide. So ... killing a kitten has to be catricide, right?

Then I say to Tristram, "You were responsible for the slugs, too, weren't you? And the prawns. And the sawn-off heel."

"Why would I do that?" Tristram is trying his best to look innocent, but he's no actor. Guilt is written all over his face.

Tink's eyes have suddenly gone narrow.

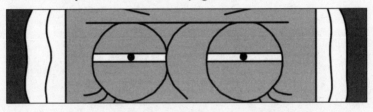

"I bet he was behind George and Felithia's bweak-up too!" she exclaims.

"What?" Tristram and I say together.

"What?" cry George and Felicia.

"Well," Tink begins, "George says Felithia dumped him."

George nods. "By text message!"

Tink carries on. "But Felithia says George dumped HER."

"He sent me an email!" Felicia protests.

"I believe the text and the email were actually sent by HIM!" declares Tink, pointing at the nutty director.

Then something truly revolting happens. Captain Quark and Galaxion do this:

Well, after that it's just a matter of unpicking Tristram's fiendish plot. It worked like this:

1
Tristram wanted to "keep it real" during the filming of ATTACK OF THE BLOBS!!! Like I said, he's a method director.

2
He roped in Rhys to help – they were at drama school together and have been friends for years, plus Tristram promised Rhys the starring role in his next movie.

3
Tristram sent the *you're dumped* messages but it was Rhys who kept inventing rumours about what Felicia or George had said and done and reporting them to the paparazzi.

Of course the whole point was for George and Felicia to hate each other enough to become real arch-enemies – which the director thought would improve the film. Then Tristram put pressure on Barry to arrange Tink's secret stunt and catnapped Woopie just so Tink would cry real tears. It was only Watson's heroism on the boat that saved Prince Rupert III from a watery grave.

Once the whole story is out in the open, it's not surprising that Felicia, George and Tink all point-blank refuse to work with Tristram or Rhys again. Both the director and Captain Quark's love interest are fired by Cosmic Films and we get an unexpected week's holiday in New York City while Zoe finds replacements for them. Me, Dad and Watson end up doing all the stuff I dreamed of – we ride in yellow taxis and go up the Empire State Building and even have a helicopter ride over the skyscrapers.

A new director is found and the film shoot goes on and on and on and then the whole thing has to be edited (which takes as long as the filming), so it's another whole year before *Attack of the Blobs!!!* hits the cinemas. When it does, it's a massive blockbuster that smashes all box-office records in its first weekend, so Dad is seriously happy. He's

CUT!

In the olden days, editing was done by literally cutting the film with a pair of scissors and sticking it together with a special kind of tape. These days it's all done digitally.

even more blissed out when the Oscar nominations are announced … and his name is on the list! We all go to the ceremony, even Gran, and it's AWESOME. We wear suits and Watson wears a diamanté collar and the four of us get to ride in a limousine and strut up the red carpet being snapped by paparazzi.

And then – get this! –
DAD WINS AN OSCAR!!!!!

So that's it. The obsessive director turned out to be the Joker, the good guy turned out to be his evil henchman and the loved-up couple got loved up all over again (YUCK!). My dad won an Academy Award, my dog rescued his arch-enemy, my best friend was reunited with her missing kitten and I turned out to be a one hundred per cent genuine superhero who flew down from the Statue of Liberty wearing a cape!

Confusing, huh? But that's the way it is in the movies!

That's a wrap!

HOW TO MAKE CONVINCING RASHES, ZITS AND PUS

DON'T TRY THIS AT HOME!

YOU WILL NEED:
- latex
- petroleum jelly
- mayonnaise or margarine
- Derma Wax
- gelatine powder
- make-up
- finely ground porridge oats or desiccated coconut
- hairdryer
- brushes
- modelling tool

RASHES

A basic rash can be created by sponging red cream blusher where required.

To make skin look as though it's peeling:

- Apply a thin layer of latex and dry with a hairdryer.
- Scratch the surface of the latex with the tip of the modelling tool.
- Tone into the rest of the skin using blusher.

To make skin look flaky:

- Apply a thin layer of latex and allow to only partially dry, then put a little porridge or coconut on top.
- Leave to dry fully.
- Blend into surrounding skin with brown and yellow cream make-up.
- To make sores ooze, apply a little petroleum jelly.

ZITS (WAX METHOD)

- Take a small piece of wax, about the size of a lentil.
- Massage until soft.
- Place it where required using modelling tool.
- Smooth around the edges to make a volcano-shaped mound.
- Colour around the edges with red cream blusher.

ZITS (LATEX METHOD)

- Apply small specks of latex to the face using the pointed end of the modelling tool.
- Dry with hairdryer.
- To increase size, apply a second layer and dry.
- Repeat until zits are the required size.
- Tone into rest of skin with red cream blusher.
- To make zits appear to have burst, apply a dash of mayonnaise or margarine to the top of each zit.

PUS

- Heat powdered gelatine and water and mix until thin and slimy. Stir in colouring to reach desired effect – use food colouring or watercolour paint.
- Be aware that gelatine stiffens when it cools.
- A good alternative is mayonnaise.

HOW TO MAKE A SIMPLE BLOOD SPURTER

DON'T TRY THIS AT HOME!

- Buy one of those novelty flower-that-squirts-water things.
- Remove the flower.
- Fill the bulb with stage blood (a few drops of red food colouring in water will do).
- Put tubing under your clothes, fixing it to your skin with sticking plasters.
- Make sure the end is in the place you want the blood to spurt from.
- Squeeze the bulb. Result!

STATUE OF LIBERTY WORKSHEET

1. Which country gave the statue to America? .... France ....

2. In what year was it given? .. 1884 ....

3. What is Lady Liberty's shoe size? ...... 879 ....

4. How large is her waist? ..... 35 ft (that's 1.07 m) ....

5. Who designed the statue? ... Frédéric-Auguste Bartholdi ....

6. Who designed the internal support structure that holds her up, and
what other landmark was he famous for designing?

.... Gustave Eiffel, who designed the Eiffel Tower in Paris ....

5. Write down the poem that is written at the feet of the statue.

... Not like the brazen giant of Greek fame ....

... With conquering limbs astride from land to land; ....

... Here at our sea-washed, sunset gates shall stand ....

... A mighty woman with a torch whose flame ....

... Is the imprisoned lightning, and her name ....

... Mother of Exiles. From her beacon-hand ....

... Glows world-wide welcome; her mild eyes command ....

... The air-bridged harbor that twin cities frame ....

... "Keep, ancient lands, your storied pomp!" cries she ....

... With silent lips. "Give me your tired, your poor, ...

... Your huddled masses yearning to breathe free, ...

... The wretched refuse of your teeming shore ....

... Send these, the homeless, tempest-tost to me, ...

... I lift my lamp beside the golden door!" ....

6. Who was the poem written by? .... Emma Lazarus ....

FILM LIST

THE PRIZE (UNCLASSIFIED)

Thriller 1963 US Colour 134 mins

Logline: Writer goes to collect prize and gets involved in Communist plot.

ALIEN 18

Sci-fi horror thriller 1979 US/UK Colour 116 mins

Logline: Alien monster is unleashed on spaceship.

GOSSIP 15

Thriller 2000 US Colour 90 mins

Logline: College students spread malicious rumour.

AMERICAN DREAMZ 12

Comedy 2006 US Colour 102 mins

Logline: Pop wannabes compete for stardom.

SCANDAL 18

Drama 1989 UK Colour 110 mins

Logline: Scandal causes downfall of government.

THE BIG SLEEP PG

Classic detective drama 1946 US BW 109 mins

Logline: Murder, blackmail, the full works.

CATS AND DOGS PG

Comedy 2001 US/Aus Colour 94 mins

Logline: Cats and dogs struggle for world domination.

THE JUNGLE BOOK U

Animated adventure 1967 US Colour 75 mins

Logline: Man-cub reared by wolves lives happily in the jungle, until an evil tiger comes looking for him.

TRAINING DAY 18

Drama 2001 US/Aus Colour 117 mins

Logline: Cop drama.

A DOG'S LIFE U

Silent comedy 1918 US BW 34 mins

Logline: Tramp and abandoned mongrel plan to steal sausages.

DEAD END 15

Horror 2003 France/US Colour 79 mins

Logline: Driving to visit relatives at Christmas, Dad takes a shortcut and sees a mysterious woman in white.

WILD WILD WEST 12

Western fantasy 1999 US Colour 101 mins

Logline: Secret agents try to stop insane inventor assassinating the President.

LETHAL WEAPON 18

Thriller 1987 US Colour 112 mins

Logline: Reckless cop and his partner bust drugs ring.

FISH TANK 15

Drama 2009 UK/Netherlands Colour 117 mins

Logline: Troubled teen's life unravels.

FILM LIST

EXTRAS 12

Comedy   2006   Poland   Colour   119 mins

Logline: Extras get hired to be in the background during the filming of a rom-com.

THE CAT'S MEOW 12

Comedy drama 2001 Ger/UK/US Colour 109 mins

Logline: Rich and famous party on a luxury yacht ends with a gunshot...

THE LOVE BUG U

Comedy   1969   US   Colour   107 mins

Logline: Herbie is a VW Beetle with a mind of his own.

TRANSFORMERS 12

Sci-fi action adventure 2007 US Colour 137 mins

Logline: Autobots and Decepticons crash-land on earth and carry on fighting.

NEW YORK, NEW YORK PG

Musical   1977   US   Colour   156 mins

Logline: Saxophonist and singer have love/hate relationship.

THE FLOWER OF EVIL 15

Mystery   2002   France   Colour   104 mins

Logline: Domestic strife in small-town France.

WIRED 18

Drama   1989   US   Colour   104 mins

Logline: Biopic about comedian and actor John Belushi.

LIBERTY STANDS STILL 15

Thriller 2002 Canada/Germany Colour 92 mins

Logline: Father takes revenge on his daughter's killer.

SECRET AGENT U

Spy thriller   1936   UK   BW   82 mins

Logline: Writer's death is faked and he is sent on a secret mission.

THE KARATE KID PG

Adventure 2010 US/China Colour 134 mins

Logline: Bullied kid learns kung fu from Jackie Chan.

KIDNAPPED U

Adventure   1971   UK   Colour   102 mins

Logline: Two Scotsmen are on the run from the wicked English.

THE INCREDIBLES U

Animation   2004   US   Colour   110 mins

Logline: Mr Incredible and family fight evil villain Syndrome.

HEAR NO EVIL 15

Thriller   1993   US   Colour   92 mins

Logline: Woman is chased by villains in pursuit of a rare coin she doesn't know she has.

CATCH THAT KID PG

Adventure 2004 US/Germany Colour 87 mins

Logline: Girl pairs up with two friends to rob bank.

THE FINAL CURTAIN 15

Drama   2002   UK/US   Colour   79 mins

Logline: Satire on TV quiz shows.

TANYA LANDMAN

Tanya has written many books for children, including the award-winning Poppy Fields murder mystery series, *Waking Merlin, Merlin's Apprentice, The Kraken Snores, The World's Bellybutton* and three stories for younger readers featuring the characters Flotsam and Jetsam.

She very much enjoys writing Sam Swann's Movie Mysteries. "I love the movies (it's hard not to when you have an actor uncle who gets eaten by a mechanical shark!*) but I've always been as interested in the backstage stuff as what's on screen. I've got two children – both boys – and two Labradors. Sam and Watson are totally based on them and what they might get up to if they were ever let loose on a film set."

Tanya also writes for young adults. You can find out more about all her books at:

www.tanyalandman.com

---

* Robert Shaw, who played Quint in *JAWS*.